# THE WITCH'S MAGIC CLOTH

BY MIYOKO MATSUTANI
ENGLISH VERSION BY ALVIN TRESSELT
ILLUSTRATED BY YASUO SEGAWA

Parents' Magazine Press • New York

copyright © 1969 by Parents' Magazine Press
All rights reserved. Printed in the United States of America
Library of Congress Catalog Card Number: 79-77787

This book was translated from Yamanbano Nishiki, originally published by
the Popular Publishing Company, Tokyo, Japan. The American edition has been
arranged through Nippon Shuppan Hanbai K.K. Tokyo.

In the days long ago there was a small village
tucked high in the mountains of Japan.
Towering behind the village was a mountain
of great height. Even on a clear day in summer
its top was always hidden in clouds.
The simple villagers believed that a wicked witch
lived up there in the clouds, and no one was so brave
or so foolish as to think of climbing the mountain.

It was the night of the full moon, and, as was the
custom in Japan, the people had gathered together
to view the moon and enjoy its beauty.

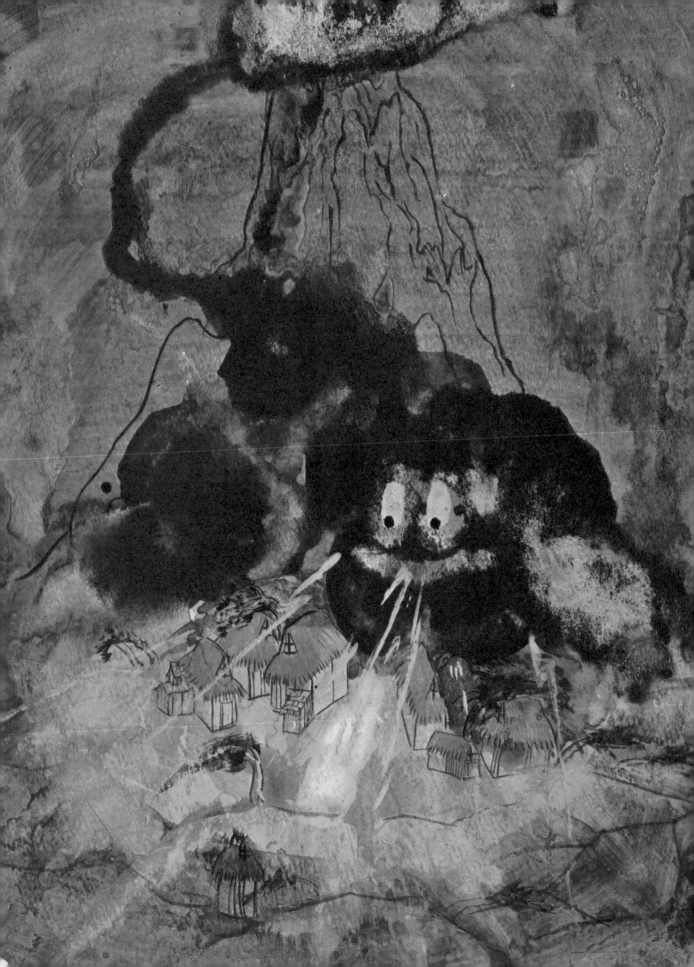

Suddenly, without warning, the sky was blotted out with fearsome black clouds. The air was filled with the crash of thunder, and great forks of lightning streaked the darkness. The people shook with fear and clung to one another, trembling like the leaves of the aspen tree.

Then a voice even louder than the thunder cried out, "The Witch of the Mountain has just given birth to her first son. She commands you to bring her fine rice cakes or she will come down and devour you all!" Then just as suddenly as the storm had come, the black clouds rolled away, and once more the night was calm, with only the pale light of the moon shining down on the frightened villagers.

The next morning the terrified people hurried about preparing rice cakes as an offering to the Witch of the Mountain. Each villager contributed a share of rice, and after working all morning they had a large pile of tender rice cakes, neatly stacked on two boards.

"Let us hope there will be enough to satisfy her hunger," they said. But then came the question—who would go up the mountain to the witch's house?

Now it so happened that in this village there were
two men named Dadahachi and Negisobe. They were
very boastful and never tired of bragging to everyone
how brave they were. The head man of the village
looked around at the gathered people. "Aha!" he said

at last. "For many years we have had to listen to Dadahachi and Negisobe tell us how fearless they are. Now is their chance to *show* us!" At once the villagers cried out in agreement, and so it was decided. The two boasters would carry the rice cakes to the witch.

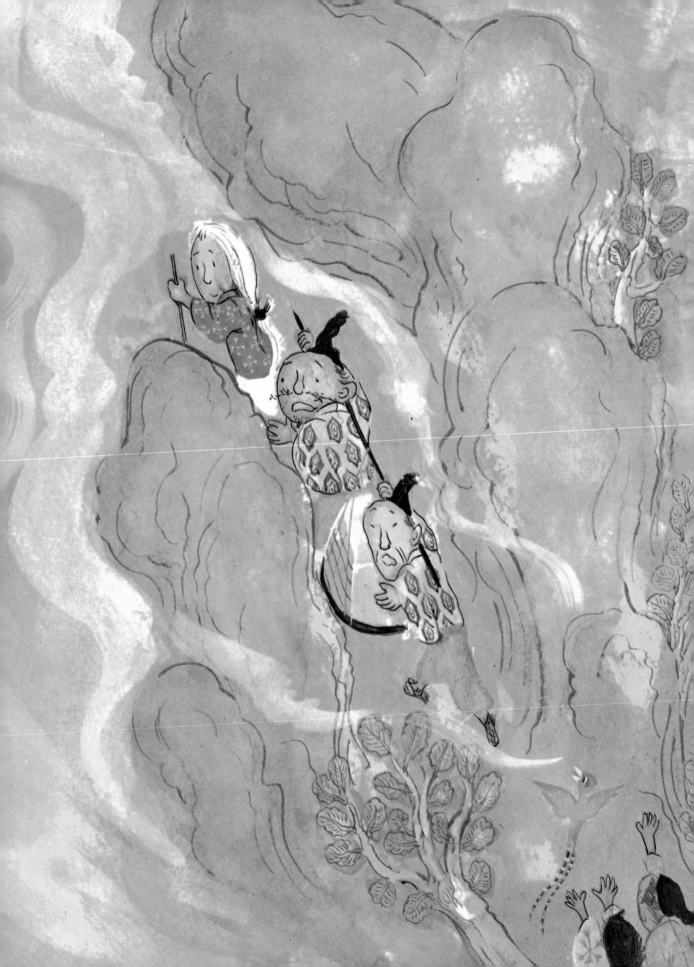

The two men looked at each other in dismay. It had been easy enough to brag and boast, but climbing the witch's mountain was something else again. "I don't really know the right path," said one.

"I'm brave enough when I know where I'm going," said the other.

"Of course," they went on, "if we had a guide to show us the way we'd be glad to take the rice cakes."

The villagers put their heads together and discussed this. True, since no one had ever climbed the mountain, who was to know what was the right way to the top?

At last an old, old woman stepped forward. "Too many years have passed over my head for me to be afraid of the witch," she said in a quavery voice. "I will help these brave men find the witch's house."

With much fear and trembling Dadahachi and Negisobe picked up the boards with the rice cakes and started up the mountain, following the old woman.

The higher they climbed the more difficult the path became. Strange wild animals peered out at them, and the men shook with fear. Coming to a clear place they looked down. "Aiyie!" they wailed. "We will never see our families and friends again!" And just then a blast of wind swept down the mountain.

"Old woman, we are surely going to be destroyed
even before we are eaten by the witch!" they cried.
The old woman just laughed. "Be brave in your hearts
and nothing can harm you," she answered. Shamed by
the woman's courage the two men pressed on.

But presently another great wind swept
down the mountain, even stronger than
the first. It blew the leaves off the trees
and sent rocks rolling down to the
valley below. The old woman grabbed
a tree root and held on with all her
strength, and soon the wind died
down. Picking herself up, she saw
that Dadahachi and Negisobe had
disappeared.

She rested awhile to catch her breath,
then said to herself, "If I return to the
village, too, the witch will surely come
down and eat us all up. If I continue
up the mountain, perhaps she will be
satisfied with eating just me. I am an
old woman and it won't much matter.
At least the village will be saved."

Having made up her mind, she tucked the
rice cakes into a safe place—as she was
not strong enough to carry them—and
continued up the mountain.

It took her many hours, for her bones
were old and weak, and she had to rest
often to regain her strength. At long
last she arrived at the entrance of a
huge hut. Sitting in the doorway was
a baby boy playing with a rock the
size of his head. "This must be the
home of the witch," she said, "and
that is her young son." She called
out in her loudest and bravest voice,
"Hello, Witch of the Mountain. I have
come from the village with rice cakes
as you commanded."

At this the matting over the doorway
was lifted and the witch herself poked
her head out. "I am so happy to see you,"
she said, smiling. "I was very hungry
last night and I sent my baby out to get
me rice cakes. I hope he didn't upset
the people of your village."

The old woman was very surprised to hear this. "Was it your newborn baby who made that great storm and cried out in such a loud voice?" she asked.
"You forget," the witch replied. "He is the son of the Mountain Witch. As soon as he was born he had the strength of ten men. But where are the rice cakes you brought?" The old woman explained
that she was too weak to carry them and
had hidden them behind a certain rock.

"I understand," said the witch kindly. "My son will get them for you. No sooner did the witch speak than the boy stood up, dashed off with the speed of the wind and was back at once with the rice cakes. "Now fetch us a bear," said his mother. "I will make bear soup and drop the rice cakes into it. I will let the old woman have some, too. She looks as if she could enjoy a good meal." In a flash the boy was back carrying a very large bear.

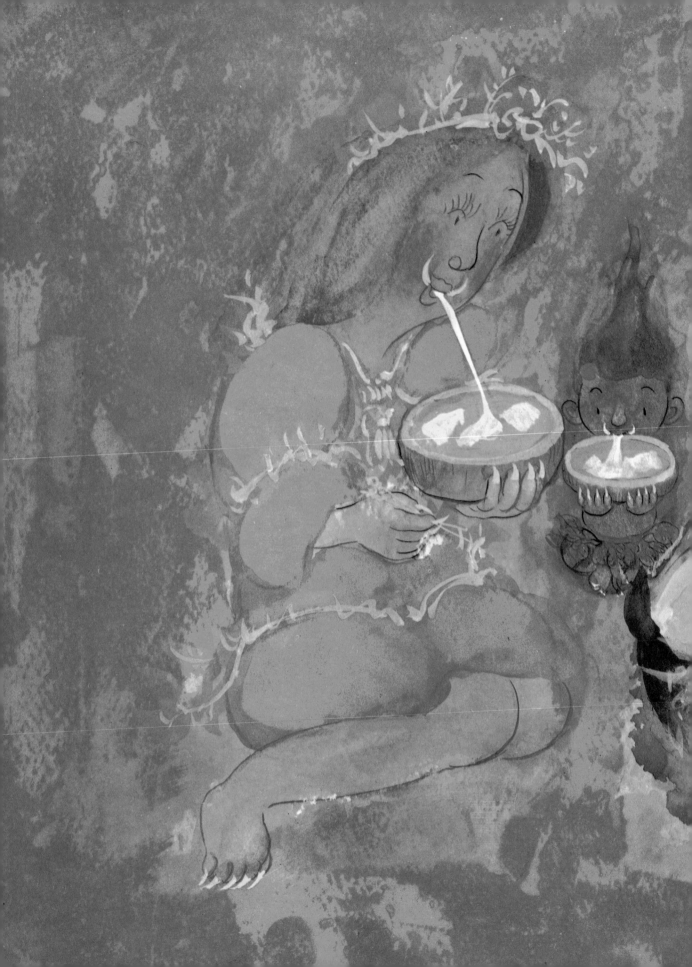

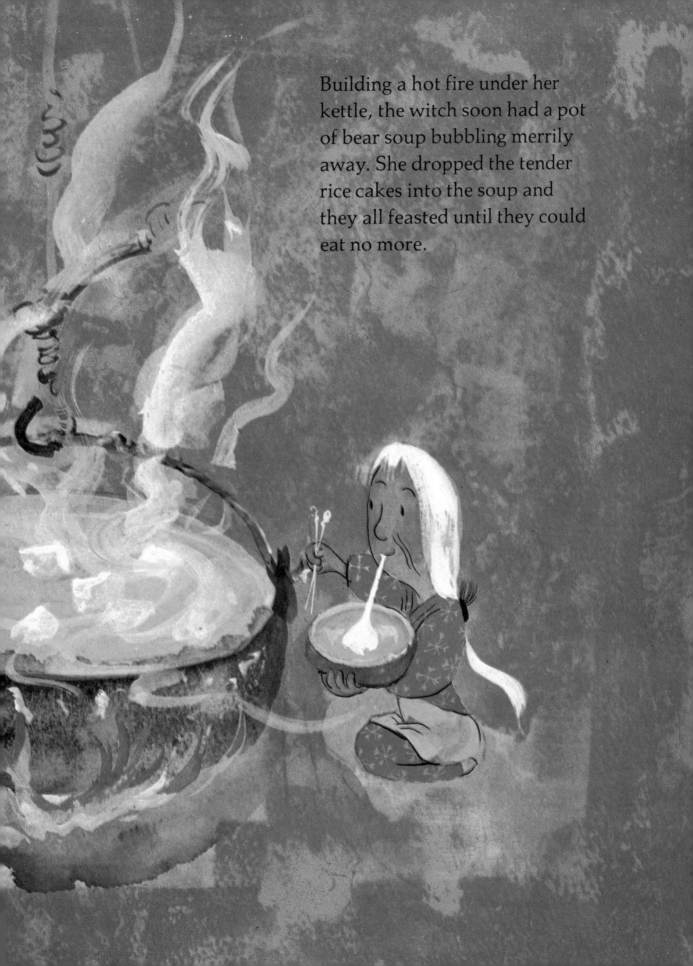

Building a hot fire under her kettle, the witch soon had a pot of bear soup bubbling merrily away. She dropped the tender rice cakes into the soup and they all feasted until they could eat no more.

When she had finished, the old woman
thanked the witch. "May I return now
to my village?" she asked.
"I would like you to stay with me for
three weeks," replied the witch. "I have
no one to help me and I still feel
weak." The old woman, fearful
that the witch might eat her,
agreed. She spent her days
fetching water and keeping
the hut clean while the
witch rested and
her little boy
played in the
dooryard.

At last the three weeks were over, and once more the old woman asked if she might return. "You have been so kind," said the witch. "Now I am strong again and you may go. I will give you a present in thanks for all you have done." With that she handed the old woman a roll of magnificent gold brocade. "This cloth will last forever," she said. "No matter how much you use, as long as you keep a small piece, the cloth will renew itself overnight. I have no gift for the people of your village," she went on, "but tell them that I will keep them always healthy."

Then the witch turned to her son. "You will carry the
old woman safely back to her village. See that no
harm comes to her."

"Oh, no!" the old woman protested. "I can find my way
down the mountain with no trouble."

But in an instant the boy had her up on his back.

"Just close your eyes tight," he said. "You will be
home in a minute."

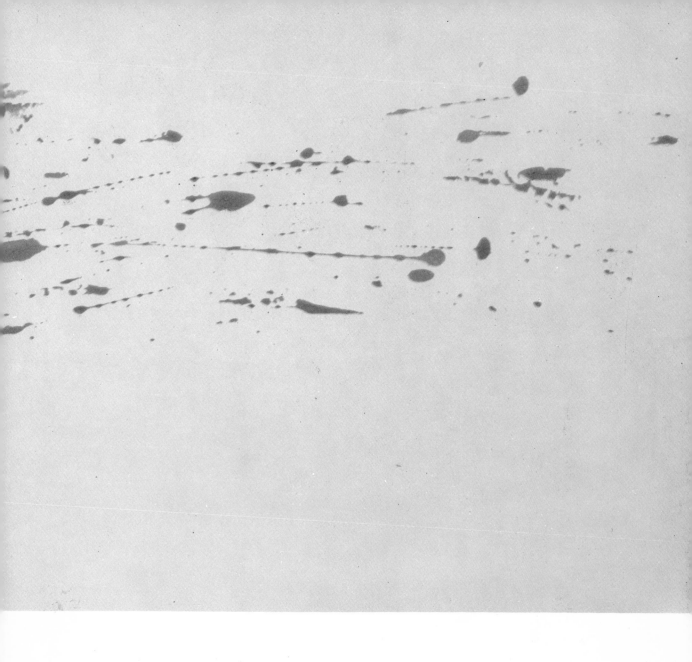

And it was just as he said. With the wind whistling
in her ears the old woman felt herself flying down
the steep mountainside, and when she opened her eyes
there she was right in front of her very own house.
"Do come in and rest before you return," she said.
But the boy had left, and in truth was already half-way
up the mountain by the time she had finished speaking.

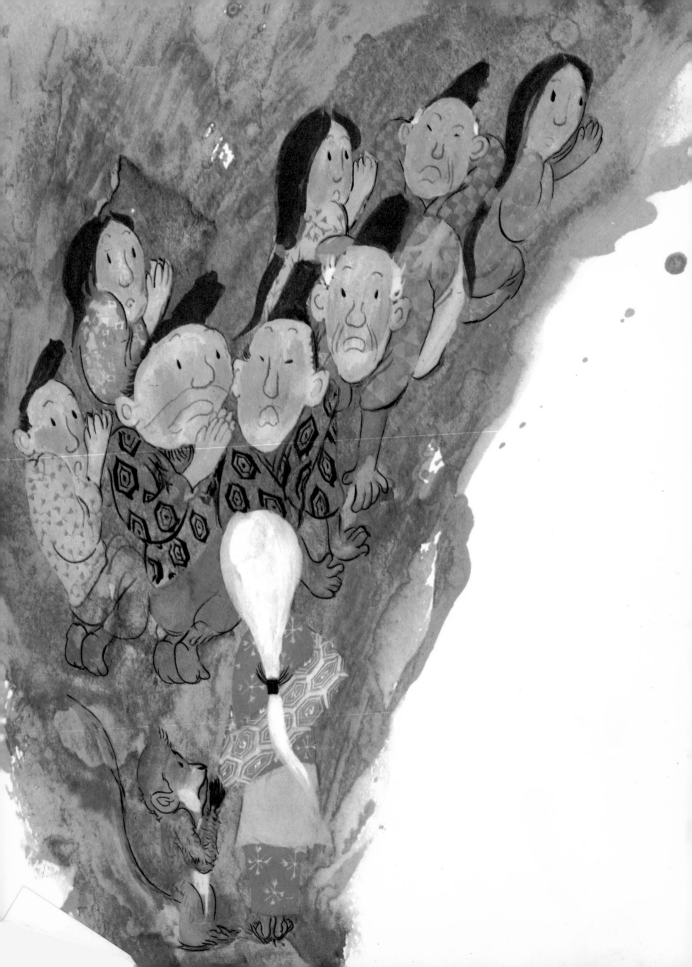

She was just about to enter her house when she heard
wailing cries inside, and the voice of the village priest
reading the prayer for the dead. She quickly went in
and demanded to know who had died. At the sight of
her everyone gasped. "A ghost!" they cried. "The spirit
of the old woman has come back to haunt us!"
"I am no ghost," she replied with a laugh. "I am the
old woman back from serving the witch." And as they all
gathered round her she told them of her adventures.

Then she showed them the roll of cloth. She quickly cut it up, giving each villager a piece, but she made certain to hold on to the last scrap. And just as the witch had said, the next morning the roll of magic cloth was as though no piece had been cut from it.

No longer did the villagers
live in fear of the witch.
They all went about dressed
in beautiful gold brocade,
and they all enjoyed the best
of health throughout their
long and happy lives—
just as the witch
had promised.